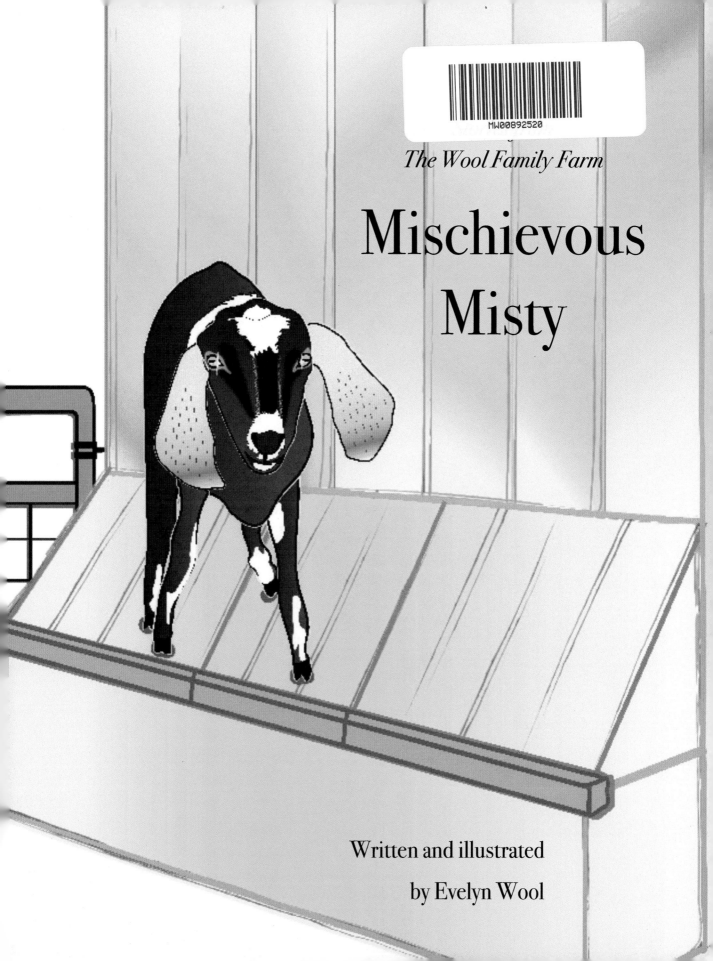

The Wool Family Farm

Mischievous Misty

Written and illustrated

by Evelyn Wool

MW00892520

Copyright © 2018 Evelyn Wool

All rights reserved. No part of this book may be transmitted or reproduced in any form or by any means, electronic or mechanical, including, but not limited to, photocopying, recording, any information storage and retrieval system, or any kind of social media—except in the case of brief quotations embodied in critical articles or reviews—without permission in writing from Evelyn Wool.

Summary: Misty is a precocious little goat who must know exactly what Gram is doing at all times. Misty's curiosity gets her into all sorts of mishaps, causing her and Gram to change their ways.

ISBN: 978-1977771919

Story, design, illustrations and layout by: Evelyn Wool

Edited by: Grace Leibolt

Technical Consultant: Hannah Wool

This paper meets the requirements of ANSI/NISO Z39.48-1992 (Permanence of Paper).
Printed in the United States of America .

For Robert, Eric, Hannah, Jennifer, and David
I love you Way Beyond the Universe
Without you, The Wool Family Farm would be just a dream

* * *

Gram knew that raising dairy goats would be a lot of work. She was prepared for the daily chores of milking, feeding, and hauling hay. She hoped that the goats would be affectionate and playful. After all, if she was going to spend so much time with them, Gram wanted to have some fun, too. She had no idea just how precocious they could be...especially Misty.

Evelyn Wool (aka Gram)

THE MEADOW

Misty was a young Nubian dairy goat who lived
in The Meadow on Gram's farm. Misty's coat was chestnut brown
with black trim. She had white patches around her nose and
on the top of her head, and a white belt around her middle.
Her long, floppy, white ears were covered in tiny brown spots
like drizzle on a rainy spring morning.

Misty had an inquisitive nature and a playful sparkle
in her eye.

When Gram asked, "Who wants to get brushed today?"
Misty would put her head in Gram's lap and stand perfectly still,
getting stroked until her fur glistened in the sunshine.

When Gram asked, "Who wants a treat?" Misty was always the first in line and would jump up on her hind legs to take a peanut.

Misty loved to be near Gram, and she always followed
her around closely ... sometimes a little too closely.

When Gram
carried water
through
The Meadow,
Misty darted
in front of her and
banged her nose
into the bucket.
Water sloshed all
over Gram's legs.

When Gram tried to pour feed into the trough,
Misty jumped up and stuck her nose in the pail.
Grain spilled all over the ground.

Gram wondered how she would ever be able to walk
through The Meadow without Misty bumping into her all the time.
Then she had an idea. Gram started singing:

It worked! When Misty heard Gram sing, she scampered
off toward the shelter with the rest of the goats.

But Misty was not always so cooperative.

Like the time Gram was standing on top of the sloped feed box, painting the goat shelter. Misty came over to see what she was doing.

"No, no, no, Misty," Gram said. "Don't jump!"

It was no use.
Misty leapt up and
started moving toward
the paint can in Gram's hand.

Misty stretched up, sticking her nose between the can and the shelter wall. She slipped and bashed into Gram, tossing her off the feed box. Gram landed with a thud on her backside.

Gram got up slowly, expecting to find paint splashed everywhere, but she didn't see any. She didn't see Misty either.

Gram peered into the shelter. Misty was hiding in the corner, shivering, with her legs clenched tightly together. Her ears and tail drooped sadly.

"What's the matter, girl? Are you hurt?" Gram asked, putting her hand on Misty's back. Misty was soaking wet!

Gram got a bucket of warm water and a clean towel. She knelt down beside Misty and gently washed the paint off her back.

Then she wrapped her arms around Misty's neck and gave her a big hug.

"You're okay, silly girl," Gram said. "You'll have to stay penned up while I finish painting."

Several days later, Gram noticed that the hay was getting low. She brought a load of fresh bales to The Meadow gate and tossed them into a pile. Then she carried them to the hay box one by one.

While Gram moved the hay,
most of the goats stayed
near the gate,
tasting the bales
left behind.

But not Misty.

Misty followed alongside Gram, pushing the hay and stepping on Gram's feet. When Gram tried to lift the bale into the hay box, Misty knocked it out of her hands.

When Gram turned back to get another bale, she saw a flash out of the corner of her eye. Misty vaulted onto the neatly stacked bales of hay.

"You don't belong in there!" scolded Gram.

That night, Gram saw how quiet the goats were at dinner time. Even Misty was too busy eating to be interested in what Gram was doing.

"Hmmm, bet I could get some chores done now without Misty getting in the way," she thought.

So, from then on,
Gram waited until
feeding time to load
hay and refill
the water bucket.

One day, Gram was busy feeding the rabbits when,
all of a sudden, the goats started hollering...

...and hollering   ...and hollering!

She glanced over
at The Meadow. Everything
looked okay, but the usually
quiet herd continued to make
noise. Gram could see Hazel
and Leah, and Georgia and
Carabel...but, where was
Misty?

Hmmm.
Something's
not right.

Gram hurried through The Meadow, eagerly looking for Misty.

"Oh, there she is, behind the hay feeder," she said aloud.

Gram looked down
    and saw Misty's head,
        buried deep in the bottom of the basket,
            twisting frantically from side to side.

Misty was stuck!

Gram held
Misty's head
and tried to
push her out.

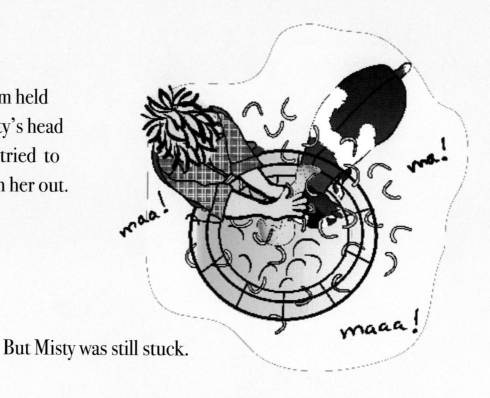

But Misty was still stuck.

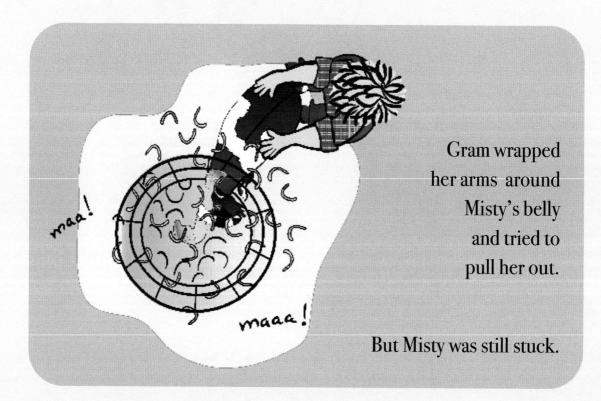

Gram wrapped
her arms around
Misty's belly
and tried to
pull her out.

But Misty was still stuck.

Gram stood
back and took
a good look
at Misty. She
noticed that her
neck was bent
in the shape
of the letter "L".

Gram pushed
Misty's body
over until it was
lined up straight
with her head.
Then she pulled
one more time.

At last,
Misty's head
popped out
of the hay feeder!

The next day, Gram watched as Misty carefully nibbled hay from the outside of the hay basket.

"Had Misty learned her lesson?" she wondered. "Or would she stick her head through the wire and get stuck again?"

Gram decided to build a new hay feeder with a heavy wire frame and metal posts. The openings in the new wire were larger and much stronger than the ones in the old basket. Now, Misty could easily get her head in and out of the feeder without getting stuck.

As time went on, Misty continued to stay near Gram and follow her around everywhere, though she was not quite as pushy as before. And whenever she heard the Dinner Time song, Misty walked next to Gram like two friends going for a stroll.

But Misty was still a curious little goat.
Every night as she drifted off to sleep, Gram
wondered what kind of mischief Misty
would get into next.

The End

Meet the Real Mischievous Misty

Yes, Misty really did knock Gram off the feed box!

Misty loves treat time.

The original hay basket.

The rebuilt hay basket.

Left to right: Georgia, Carabel, Hazel, Leah, and Misty. Vivi (in the background), is Gram's guard llama.

Gram's favorite part of the day is spending time with her goats.

Dairy Goat Breeds

Alpine Medium-large sized goat with upright ears and long neck. Usually white or cream color with black or dark trim, may also have spots. Notably intelligent and can be especially assertive.

LaMancha Medium sized goat with very small ears that look like cauliflower. Can be any color pattern. Especially calm and gentle.

Nigerian Dwarf Miniature sized goat in any color pattern, with upright, pointy ears. Friendly and vocal goats.

Nubian Large sized goat with long, floppy ears, and a rounded (Roman) nose. Any color pattern. Sociable and outgoing. Can be particularly stubborn. Milk has highest butterfat content.

Oberhasli Medium sized goat with upright ears. Reddish brown with black trim or all black.

Saanen Large sized, all-white goat with upright, pointy ears. Typically sweet-natured and quiet. Heaviest milker.

Toggenburg Small-medium sized goat with upright ears. Long, shaggy coat in fawn, silver or chocolate with white or cream belly and legs.

The Dinner Time Song

This is the song that Gram made up to sing to Misty.
Can you sing The Dinner Time Song? Maybe your mom, dad,
or teacher can play it for you on the piano. Can you learn how to
play it yourself?

What song would you make up for Misty?

Glossary

Which word do you think best describes Misty?

Affectionate
[uh-fek-shuh-nit]

Readily feeling or showing tenderness. *Is Misty affectionate? How about Gram?*

Cooperative
[koh-op-er-uh-tiv]

Willing to be helpful by doing what someone wants or asks for. *Is there a time in the story when Misty is cooperative?*

Inquisitive
[in-kwiz-i-tiv]

Unduly curious, prying, nosy. *When is Misty inquisitive?*

Mischievous
[mis-chuh-vuh s]

Able or tending to cause annoyance, trouble, or minor injury. *Can you name two times in the story when Misty is mischievous?*

Persistent(ly)
[per-sis-tuh nt]

Lasting or enduring. Refusing to give up. *What does Misty do persistently? Why?*

Precocious
[pri-koh-shuh s]

Forward, intelligent, clever, quick. *How does Misty show she is clever?*

Vault(ed)
[vawlt]

To jump over an object in a single movement. *What does Misty vault onto?*

Mischievous Misty Fan Club

Did you like the story of Mischievous Misty? Would you like to learn more about the real Misty? If so, be sure to get your mom or dad's permission, then scan the QR code, or type the URL into an internet browser. Enter the password: Misty.

TheWoolFamilyFarm.com/FanClub

The Misty Fan Club page is loaded with goodies specially made for owners of this book. Misty fans will be able to:

- Print free coloring and activity pages
- Watch Misty eating dinner
- Hear Gram sing The Dinner Time Song
- Ask Gram a question
- Purchase the official Mischievous Misty Activity Book (help feed Misty for a day)

Welcome to the club!

Stories from
The Wool Family Farm

We spent years visiting all types of farms: cattle and dairy farms, pig and sheep and goat farms, dreaming of the day we would start our own. By the time we found our very own thirty-one acre slice of paradise—complete with house, barn, cabin and chickens—we were excited and ready to dive right in. All we needed to do was build a few fences and bring on the livestock. Piece of cake.

What could possibly go wrong?

* * *

From curious goats to runaway cows, noisy lambs to nosy donkeys, follow along as Gram — and Gramps — make the journey from city folk to farmers. Be on the lookout for future story books. You never know what will happen next!

Draw your favorite picture of Misty

Draw your favorite farm animal

Made in the USA
Columbia, SC
24 June 2022

62133787R00024